THE RICH MAN
AND THE SINGER
Folktales from Ethiopia

TOLD BY MESFIN HABTE-MARIAM

EDITED AND ILLUSTRATED BY

CHRISTINE PRICE

E. P. DUTTON & CO., INC. NEW YORK

Other Books by Christine Price

Published simultaneously in Canada by Clarke,
Irwin & Company Limited, Toronto and Vancouver

SBN: 0-525-38224-0   LCC: 73-102738

Printed in the U.S.A.   First Edition

THIS BOOK IS FOR

JOSEPH

Contents

(All the stories are Amharic tales except those for which other sources are noted.)

THE RICH MAN
AND THE SINGER

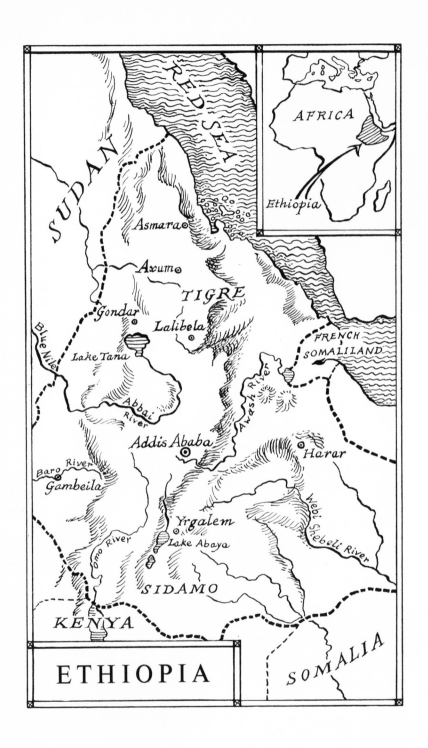

SUDAN

RED SEA

AFRICA

Ethiopia

Asmara

Axum

TIGRE

Gondar

Lalibela

Lake Tana

FRENCH
SOMALILAND

Blue Nile

Abbai
River

Awash River

Addis Ababa

Harar

Baro River

Gambeila

Webi Shebeli River

Yrgalem

Omo River

Lake Abaya

SIDAMO

KENYA

ETHIOPIA

SOMALIA

The World of the Stories

The heart of Ethiopia is a high tableland, broken by rugged mountains, deep-carved gorges, and strange, flat-topped hills.

In the spring, the time of the Small Rains, pillars of white cloud tower in the sky and cast their shadows over the open pastures where cattle graze. Clumps of trees shelter the farms and the villages of round, thatched houses, and in the fields nearby people are at work on the threshing floors. They drive teams of oxen in endless circles over the cut grain, and separate the chaff by winnowing, tossing up showers of grain into the wind with long wooden scoops.

Riders move across the broad land between the villages, their clothes brilliantly white against the green and fawn of the earth. The harnesses of their horses are decked with silver and with long strips of leather and swinging red tassels. One rider may have two or three retainers to run at his side, and an important person will canter along under an umbrella with a train of ten men strung out behind him.

Everywhere there are people walking. Lines of small, white-clad figures trail over the distant hillsides, and along the road people are walking to market with goods to sell—stiff, folded hides balanced on their heads and baskets of chickens and eggs on carrying poles.

1

Women in white dresses swing along with an easy step, holding up colored umbrellas against the sun. Men and boys drive strings of trotting pack-donkeys or herds of cattle with magnificent upswept horns. Some of the men are walking to their work in the fields, but others may be on a journey of many days, bound for a village beyond the horizon.

These people are the Amhara, and the high country where they live is the setting for most of the stories in this book. The people of Ethiopia are as varied as their land. Those who live in the cool uplands speak different languages and follow different customs and religious beliefs from the dwellers in the scorched deserts or the tropical river valleys.

The Amhara and the people of Tigré, in the northern part of the country, are Christians of the Ethiopian Orthodox Church. The Amharic language is the language of government in Addis Ababa, the capital city, which lies in the center of the land. South of the capital live the Guragé people and the Gallas, most of whom are Muslims, while in the province of Sidamo, on the southern border, many of the people follow an ancient religion of spirit-worship. They pay homage to the spirits of nature, of fire, and of water.

Sidamo is greener and warmer than the land to the north, and there are no large towns. The people herd their cattle and spotted goats on high grasslands and along the shores of lakes. The men go armed with spears, and their wives wear dresses of brown leather and strings of bright blue beads. Their dome-shaped houses, set in gardens of false-banana trees, are thatched with grass or covered with a smooth armor of split bamboo that gleams like metal in the sun.

Tales told in Sidamo about fierce cannibal monsters

2

have a more fantastic flavor than the Amharic stories. Yet folktales in Ethiopia are often passed from one group of people to another, and it is hard to tell the true home of a story that turns up in several different places.

Tales from other lands have also found their way to Ethiopia. Some were brought in by African people from the south and west, but many others can be traced to more distant countries. Stories are the easiest of all baggage for travelers to carry, and throughout its long history Ethiopia has seen the coming and going of many travelers.

Two thousand years ago, when the ancient town of Axum was the capital of an Ethiopian empire, its merchants went forth to trade with Egypt, Arabia, and India. Travelers from Syria brought Christianity to Ethiopia in the fourth century A.D. In the seventh century the Christian emperor of Axum welcomed people of the Muslim faith—the first followers of the Prophet Muhammad. Both Christians and Muslims linked Ethiopia with the countries of the Middle East. Pilgrims, scholars, and traders passed to and fro between Ethiopia and Jerusalem, Mecca, and the rich exciting lands of *The Arabian Nights*.

The Ethiopian Christians in the Middle Ages were great builders. Their churches and monasteries were centers of learning for the *temaris,* the wandering students whose adventures were the theme of many tales. Some of the churches were not built with stone upon stone but carved out of the rock of the mountainsides, like colossal sculptures. The mountain village of Lalibela is famous today for its wonderful rock-cut churches, carved there in the thirteenth century when the little town was a royal capital and a holy place of Christian pilgrimage.

3

When a new capital, called Gondar, was founded four hundred years later, travelers from Europe had come to Ethiopia, the first in a long line of missionaries, explorers, and soldiers. Gondar was a splendid walled city. Stories are still told about the kings who ruled there, and we can still see the grand stone castles they lived in.

Europe, the Middle East, and the countries of Asia—all have contributed stories to the stock of the Ethiopian storytellers. But these borrowed ideas were put into Ethiopian dress. The storytellers wove their tales around the familiar animals and people of their own land. Through their stories we meet farmers and kings; wise men and thieves; the lordly lion and the fierce leopard; the clever baboon and the greedy hyena.

Above all, the stories show us the wisdom and the deep beliefs of the people. Storytelling in Ethiopia is a way of teaching. Mothers tell the old folktales to their children at home to teach them what things are most important in life—honesty and tact, respect for others and trust in God.

From these tales we learn that the weak can conquer the strong, that the poor man can be wiser than his rich neighbor, and that the small, quick-witted man—or animal—can triumph over the big, powerful one. Quarrels are settled by battles of words instead of blows, and the shrewd judgment of the baboon is more respected than the teeth of the leopard or the hyena.

We may hear the cry of the hyena and a burst of barking from the village dogs as we sit down to listen to a storyteller. It is a cold, windy night in the highlands, but the fire is bright and warm. The cattle are safely gathered in, and the day's work is done. The storyteller is ready with a tale. . . .

The Rich Man and the Singer

Once there lived a rich man in a magnificent house. He was a merchant and he had a great deal of money. There were many servants in his house, and he had a big herd of cattle and the finest white horses for riding. He was not a bad man either, for every day he gave money to the beggars who came crowding to his gate.

People envied and respected the rich man and thought he must be the happiest person in the world. Each night he had nothing to do but count his gold and jewels—and listen to songs.

The songs came from a small, shabby cottage next

door to the rich man's grand house. A poor shoemaker lived there, the poorest person in the town. He lived from hand to mouth, and sometimes there was not a crumb of food in his house and he slept without dinner. But this did not make the shoemaker sorry for himself. He had the gift of song.

When he came home from work, he would sing and sing until he was too tired to sing anymore, and his songs were the sweetest ever heard.

Now as the rich man listened to him, night after night, he could not understand how the shoemaker could sing so sweetly when he was so poor. At last he summoned the shoemaker and said to him: "You seem to be so happy in your poverty! I listen to your joyful songs every night. Tell me, what is the reason for your happiness?"

"It is true that I am very poor," answered the shoemaker, "but I can forget my misery by singing. The songs make me happy."

"I am not at all happy," the rich man said, "in spite of all my gold and jewels, my cattle and horses and servants. How would you like to be as rich as I am?"

The shoemaker could hardly believe what he heard, and he said he would like it very much.

"Then give me your skill in singing," said the rich man, "and I will give you all my riches."

The shoemaker agreed quickly, before the rich man had time to regret what he had said, and the exchange was made. The rich man gave the shoemaker the great house, the servants, the cows and horses and all the jewels and gold, and he went to live in the little thatched cottage next door. Soon he became an even better singer than the shoemaker. Every night he sang for hours on end until he was so weary he fell into a deep and happy sleep.

But the shoemaker in the big house slept hardly a wink.

Every night he would sit up late, counting his gold and diamonds. When at last he lay down to sleep, he would spend the whole night wracking his brain to think of new ways to make more money. If he slept at all, he would wake in fear and trembling at the smallest sound. Even the scuttle of a mouse might be the footfall of a thief!

He never smiled. When he rode out on his fine white horse, he never spoke with his neighbors. He was afraid they might rob him of his wealth.

As the shoemaker grew richer and richer, he grew more and more miserable.

At last he could bear it no longer. He stuffed a bag full of gold and silver, threw it on his shoulder, and went to the rich man in the little cottage next door.

"Here, take your wealth!" he cried, and he tossed the bag on the earthen floor. "When you took away my skill in singing, you robbed me of my happiness too! Take back your wealth, I beg you, and give me back my happiness!"

So the rich man took back his wealth, and the shoemaker went to live again in his little cottage. Every night, as the rich man counted his money, he heard the songs of the shoemaker, more joyful and more beautiful than ever. The shoemaker was poor again, and sometimes he went to bed hungry, but he was the happiest man in the town.

When the people saw him so happy they were glad and they said: "Happiness is better than wealth."

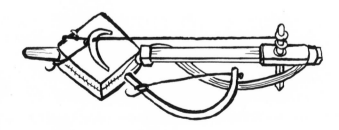

The Farmer and the Leopard

Once a leopard was being chased by hunters. While he was running for his life he met a farmer and begged to be saved from the hunt.

The farmer took pity on the leopard and hid him in a *silicha,* the big leather bag that the farmer used for carrying grain. He had just tied up the top of the bag when the hunters came galloping by.

"Where is the leopard?" they shouted. "Have you seen the leopard?"

"No," said the farmer. "I have seen no leopard."

So away went the hunters, and after they had gone, the

farmer opened the bag and freed the leopard. But as soon as the leopard got out, he turned on the farmer.

"I am hungry!" he snarled. "I am going to eat you!"

"But I saved you from the hunters," said the farmer. "You can't eat me!"

"I am hungry! I need to eat!" said the leopard.

"But I saved your life!"

"I shall die," said the leopard, "if I don't eat!"

"Well, before you eat me," said the farmer, "let us take our case to judges. If they decide you should eat me, so be it! I shall be eaten."

So they went in search of judges.

First they found the gazelle, grazing by the river. She took one look at the fierce leopard and she said: "Oh, no, there is nothing to stop the leopard from eating the man. If the leopard is hungry, he must have food."

Then the jackal listened to the case, and then the hyena and the hare and the monkey; and they all looked at the fierce leopard and quickly agreed with the gazelle. "If the leopard is hungry, he must eat the man at once!"

The last to hear the case was the baboon. She listened carefully, and then she said to the farmer and the leopard: "I must know exactly what happened before I can pass judgment on your case. Will you first show me how the leopard was hidden in the bag?"

The farmer and the leopard agreed to do this, and the leopard got back into the farmer's bag.

"Now," said the baboon, "how was it that you tied the bag? Show me how you did that!"

So the farmer tied the bag firmly at the top.

"Now," said the baboon, "this is my judgment. Farmer, use your stick before you are eaten up!"

The farmer understood what she meant, and he beat the bag with all his might until the leopard was dead.

Mammo the Fool

Mammo was the son of a poor old woman. His mother earned her living by selling the thin, flat bread called *injera,* and also *tella,* which is barley beer.

Although Mammo was her only son, she was always angry with him because he was so foolish. Everyone in the village called him "Mammo the Fool." Whenever his mother sent him out on an errand, the village children would gather together and shout at him, "Fool! Fool!"

But Mammo never minded that. He used to stop and shout and laugh with them, quite forgetting what his mother had ordered him to do.

One day she sent him to the nearby market to buy butter. He went to the market as he had been told, did his buying, and began the journey home.

The butter was in a small cup with a leaf for a cover. Mammo was carrying it in his hands when the children began to mock him as usual, and one of the older boys shouted: "Mammo, why are you holding the butter that way? Throw away the leaf and the cup and put the butter on your head! That's the way you should carry it!"

Mammo thought for a moment and then did as he was told. As it was midday and the sun was very hot, the butter soon melted and ran down his face. Mammo reached home empty-handed, and his mother was very angry. She demanded to know where he had lost the butter, and when he told her what had happened, she beat him.

"You should have carried the butter in your hands," she said, "not on your head!"

Next day she sent Mammo to bring home a cat from the house of a neighbor. So off he went and fetched the cat, but remembering what his mother had said, he held the cat tightly in his hands. The poor creature struggled and scratched and spat until Mammo's hands were torn and bleeding. At last he had to let her go.

He went home without the cat but with blood pouring from his fingers. His mother gave him another beating and said, "You should have pulled the cat along on the end of a string!"

Some days passed before Mammo's mother sent him on another errand. This time he was to bring meat from the butcher's. Mammo went and fetched the meat as he had been told. Then he tied the meat on the end of a piece of string and began to drag it along the road, because his mother had beaten him for not dragging the cat!

11

Soon there was a whole crowd of people marching along with him, laughing and mocking and calling to their neighbors to come out and see. All the village children were there, and all the dogs in the neighborhood came running at the smell of the meat.

But Mammo was sure he was doing right. When he reached home, he proudly handed the meat to his mother. But what meat! Only a little bit of bone was left; the village dogs had eaten all the rest.

Mammo's mother beat him even harder than before. "You foolish boy," she cried, "why did you drag the meat? You ought to have carried it on your back!"

A few days later, Mammo's mother told him to take the donkey to the pasture. Mammo remembered her advice, and with all his strength he heaved the donkey onto his back and started out along the road.

Now a young girl was watching from her window, and when she saw Mammo plodding off with the donkey on his back, she began to laugh. She laughed so hard she almost fainted. At the sound of her laughter, her parents came running to her room, and suddenly they heard her say, "Look at that foolish fellow with the donkey on his back!"

The parents were astonished to hear their daughter talk, for she had suffered a dreadful sickness that had made her speechless for seven years. The father was so happy that his daughter could talk again that he ran out and called Mammo to come in. There and then, with the daughter's consent, Mammo was given her hand in marriage.

So Mammo the Fool was married and lived happily with his wife. But now he was Prince Mammo, for the young girl he had cured of her sickness was a beautiful princess.

The Clever Baboon

Once a hyena and a baboon went to the house of the lion to be hired as servants.

They found the lion in a fierce and hungry mood. He glared down at them and demanded to know why they had come. The two animals saluted him humbly, and the baboon explained that they wished to be his servants. In return for their work they asked for his protection, and also—for the hyena—a few bones left over from the lion's meals.

As the lion was hungry and wanted to go hunting, he agreed quickly to take the two animals into his service.

13

He told them what to do and hurried off to the forest.

The lion soon found a gazelle beside the river. He pounced on her and killed her and ate until he was full. All that remained were the hide and the bones. He picked them up and carried them home to his servants.

The baboon and the hyena were cleaning the house. The lion showed them what he had brought. The hyena's mouth began to water when he saw the bones, but the lion gave the bones and hide to the baboon.

"Baboon," said the lion, "you may take care of the bones. As for the hide, you must use that to make me some fine new shoes. Make them as quickly as you can, or I shall eat you!"

The baboon promised to do as she was told. The lion was satisfied and lay down to sleep off his meal. He was soon asleep and snoring.

"Please, baboon," said the hyena, "give me just a mouthful of those wonderful bones."

The baboon gave him just a mouthful and hung the rest of the bones from the branch of a tree, too high for him to reach. Then the baboon looked at the hide and trembled with fright. How was she to make shoes for the lion? She had never made shoes in her life!

When several days had passed and the hide had grown hard and dry, the baboon dragged it down to the river. There she soaked the hide in the water until it was soft and pliable, ready to be made into shoes. But she did not know how to make shoes, and the lion would eat her! The only way to be safe was to kill the lion. But how?

Then suddenly, while she was soaking the hide, the baboon saw her face in the water. That gave her an idea.

She picked up the hide and ran back to the house. The lion was lying in the sun outside. "Where have you been?" he roared. "Where are my new shoes?"

"O master!" said the baboon, trembling all over. "I was soaking the hide in the river, when I had such a terrible fright! There in the water I saw a huge and powerful lion! He was even bigger than you are!"

The lion let out a mighty roar. "A lion in the river!" he said. "I don't believe it!"

"But it's true!" cried the baboon. "I have never seen such a terrible lion!"

The lion stood up, switching his tail from side to side. "Very well," he said, "you show me this terrible lion. But I warn you—if he isn't there, I shall eat you!"

So the two of them went down to the river, and the baboon took the lion to a place where the water was very deep and dark. "Now," she said, "look down into the river and see if I told you the truth."

Snarling and switching his tail, the lion looked over the edge. There, deep in the water, he saw a terrible lion snarling back at him—the fiercest and most terrible lion he had ever seen! The lion leaped into the water to seize the stranger by the throat. There was a mighty SPLASH! and he was gone forever.

The baboon went back to the lion's house, feeling safe at last. "How good it would be," she thought, "if I could have this fine house all to myself, instead of sharing it with that nasty hyena!"

Then she saw the hide of the gazelle drying in the sun. That gave her an idea.

Next day, when the hyena asked her where their master had gone, she told him the lion was away on a visit.

"Then please give me the rest of the bones," said the hyena. "I am so hungry!"

"Very well," said the baboon, "if you will agree to two conditions. First of all, you must be blindfolded before you start eating."

"Ha! I don't mind that," said the hyena. "Once I crack those bones with my teeth, they will taste just as good whether I see them or not!"

"My second condition," said the baboon, "will give you no trouble at all. You are such a fine, brave animal. You can endure pain without flinching, I am sure."

"What sort of pain?" asked the hyena.

"Oh, just a few needle-pricks in your tail," said the baboon.

The hyena laughed. "Is that all? Quick, my friend, put on the blindfold and give me the bones!"

So the baboon put on the blindfold and gave him a few of the bones. Then she took needle and thread and began quietly sewing the dried hide of the gazelle to the hyena's tail.

At the first pricks of the needle he yelped. "Stop that!" he said. "You are spoiling my meal!"

"Remember our agreement," said the baboon. "No bones without this little pain in your tail!"

"Oh, very well," said the hyena.

The baboon gave him another bone and went on stitching. She only fed him if he kept quiet. At the smallest squeak of pain she pushed the bones away.

"I am most surprised," she said, "to see a big, brave animal like you objecting to a little pain. Perhaps you are not as brave as I thought you were."

16

"The pain is nothing," growled the hyena, and he crunched another mouthful of bones. "You are tickling me—that's all!"

He had barely eaten the last scrap when the baboon finished her sewing, bit off the thread, and cried out: "Hyena, the lion is coming! And you've eaten all the bones! He'll kill us when he sees what we've done. Quick! run for your life!"

And with that, the baboon raced away, scrambled up a tree, and shouted from the top: "Run, hyena, run!"

The hyena sprang to his feet and ran. But the blindfold was still on his eyes, and the dried hide sewn to his tail went bumping and rattling behind him over the rocks. The hyena thought it was the lion. The lion was close on his tail! And the hyena ran on and on, dragging the hide behind him, until at last he tumbled into a deep gully and lay dead at the bottom.

Thus the clever baboon got rid of the lion and the hyena and lived by herself as mistress of the house.

The Husband Who Wanted
to Mind the House

Once there lived a man and his wife who were always arguing about household affairs. The husband was a farmer, and one day, when he came home from his work in the fields, he found his wife still preparing the food for their meal. He was very hungry, and he began to blame his wife for being so late.

"You are always late!" he cried. "You don't do things the way you should. Your work is much easier than mine, but you can't do it properly."

18

At this the woman became angry. "You are quite wrong about my work," she said. "I believe *your* work is easier than mine!"

So a fierce argument broke out between them, and neither one would give way. They argued until they were hoarse and breathless, and at last the woman said: "If you think that a woman's work is so easy, why don't you try it? Tomorrow I will do your tasks and you do mine."

The man agreed, and he sat down to his meal feeling quite pleased with himself. He was sure he had picked the easier job.

Next morning each began the other's work. The woman took her husband's stick in her hand and said to him: "Now I am going to the farm. You must be sure to bring me something to eat at midday, as I have always done for you."

So she drove the oxen to the farm, yoked them to the plow, and started to do the plowing. She had no difficulty at all.

The man, left at home, began his job as a housewife. In the morning he milked the cows in their fenced enclosure, and that was easy enough. He felt so pleased with himself that he forgot to fasten the gate in the fence when he took the milk into the house.

He put the small jar of milk on the floor and started to cook some cabbage for dinner. He put plenty of cabbage into the pot. His wife, he thought, never used to cook enough! He had just got the pot boiling when he heard a terrible noise outside. Shouting and screaming and mooing of cattle! He ran outside to see what was the matter.

The cows had got out! They had scattered all over the neighbors' gardens and were eating cabbages and carrots and every vegetable in sight! The neighbors were in a

19

terrible rage. The poor man ran up and down waving his arms and shouting and beating the cows with a stick. At last he managed to get them back to the gateway in the fence. He drove them inside and slammed and bolted the gate. He sank down exhausted while the neighbors raged at him until they were hoarse.

When they finally went back to their houses, the man had a moment of peace and quiet, until suddenly—he began to smell a terrifying smell!

He sprang to his feet. Black smoke was pouring out of his kitchen. He rushed inside. The cabbage had boiled dry and was burned to a cinder, his wife's best cooking pot was ruined, and the jar of milk lay empty on the floor. The cats had got in and drunk up all the milk!

The man was so weary it took him a long time to find another pot and put on some more cabbage to boil. He quite forgot about taking food to his wife in the field. Suddenly his wife came storming into the house.

"Why didn't you bring me any food?" she cried. "I have been plowing in the field all the morning and I am hungry! Where is the dinner? If woman's work is so easy, why are you so slow?"

The poor man had not even the strength to argue with her. "Please forgive me," he said. "I was wrong. Let me go back to my plowing. Your work is *much* harder than mine."

"And yet it looked so easy," said the woman, "just as playing the drum looks easy—when some one else is doing it!"

The Women Who Wanted
to Govern the Land

People say that once upon a time women rose up against men. The women said that men were prejudiced against them.

"We are oppressed and downtrodden," they declared. "We are only allowed to attend to household affairs— otherwise we are completely ignored!"

They discussed this among themselves, getting more and more angry, and decided to go to court and protest. So off they went in a body.

When they reached the court, they were welcomed by the noblemen and the high officials of the government, who politely asked the reason for their coming.

"We are protesting," said the women. "We have never been given any responsibilities but minding the house and cooking and bringing up children! We want to have great responsibilities and important work to do, as you have! We want all sorts of positions in the government! We are no weaker than you! Give us your work and we will do it as well as you do!"

The high officials and the noblemen listened to the demands of the women and they were much surprised. They said they must have time to discuss the matter privately, and so they did.

On one thing the men were all agreed. They said the women could not possibly be trusted to run the government, for what did women know about the law and the court procedure? But the trouble was that if the men did not meet the women's demands, the women could make their lives miserable at home. Husbands would be henpecked. Wives might even refuse to cook the meals or mind the children. So what was to be done?

At last the high officials and the noblemen hit on a plan. They called the women before them and said: "You must go to the king's palace. Only the king can decide whether your request should be granted. But we are going to give you a heavy responsibility. You are to deliver a secret message to the king. The message is enclosed in this box, which must on *no* account be opened."

So the high officials and the noblemen gave the women a small box, tightly closed, and sent them on their way to the king's palace.

The women were proud to have such a responsibility and they carried the box with care. But as they journeyed on and on—for it was a long road to the king's palace—they grew more and more curious about what was in the box. Some thought they heard strange sounds coming from inside. Others said they heard no such thing. At last they decided to take a quick look in the box to find out who was right.

"Just a quick look would do no harm," they said. "The king will never know."

So gently and carefully they opened the box—and out burst a beautiful golden bird! They sprang to catch it, but the bird flew up and away, high in the sky.

The women were terrified. They did not know what to do. Then one of them noticed that there was a sealed letter lying in the bottom of the box. "Look! the secret message is safe!" she cried. "The king will never know about the bird!"

So the women closed the box and went on their way with joy. When they reached the palace, the king received them graciously, opened the box, and read the letter.

Then he looked down from his throne at the women and spoke in a voice like thunder: "This letter tells me you were to bring me a bird of great rarity and beauty. Where is that bird?"

Then the women knew they had no escape. They confessed what they had done.

The king looked at them severely. "You have broken your promise," he said. "You have not obeyed orders. How can we give you great responsibilities when you cannot even bear a small one?"

And the women had nothing to say. All they could do was go back to their cooking.

The Farmer and the King

Once upon a time a certain king went hunting with a large company of people. They were hunting elephants, for in those days, long ago, killing an elephant was a grand and heroic thing to do.

The king and his people set out from Gondar, the royal capital city, and after riding for several days they came to a great forest. There it happened that the king lost his way. He had ridden on ahead of the others and suddenly found himself alone. He looked for his courtiers and his soldiers and they looked for him; but all in vain.

The king did not know which way to take to go back to

24

Gondar. So he took the way he guessed was right. He rode fast, hoping to find his people, but after many hours he still had not found them. At last, when he was too weary to travel any farther, the king saw a farmer going home from work.

"Which is the way to Gondar?" the king called out to him. "I am a hunter and I have lost my way in the forest!"

The farmer said that Gondar was two days' journey from there, and seeing that the king was weary, he took him home. He gave the king good hospitality, with a fine meal and a bed for the night, and in the morning he told him which way to take to Gondar.

"I would be glad," said the king, "if you would come with me to Gondar, for I am a stranger in this part of the land and I might lose my way. Besides," he added, "I am a rich man. I will reward you when we reach the city."

The farmer agreed, and they set out together, both of them riding the king's horse. As they journeyed on, the farmer said: "Do you live in Gondar?"

"Yes, I do," said the king.

"Then would you do me a favor, please?" said the farmer.

"Of course, my friend."

"Then show me the king," said the farmer, "for in all my life I have never seen him."

The king agreed to do so, as soon as they came to Gondar.

When they were about an hour's ride from the city, the king said to the farmer: "It is very easy to tell the king from other men. Just remember one thing: *he does not do what others do.* Watch carefully and you will be sure to see him."

An hour later they reached the palace. A great crowd of people was gathered at the gate, already mourning

25

over the disappearance of the king. When they saw him coming, they broke into cheers and rejoicings.

The farmer could not understand it at all. "Where are we?" he asked.

The king explained that the building in front of them was the royal palace, and at that moment the gates were flung open. "Now we shall go inside," he said, "and you will see the king."

As they rode in through the gate, the farmer asked how he would know the king among all the distinguished people who were lined up to greet them in front of the palace.

"You will see him," said the king, "among those guardsmen on horseback over there. Watch for one thing, as I told you before. *He does not do what others do.* He will not get down from his horse when the others get down from their horses to salute him."

By now they had reached the band of guardsmen, who sprang from their horses and knelt down to give the king their salutation. The only men still on horseback were the farmer and the king, one behind the other on the king's horse.

The crowd of people gazed at them in amazement. They had never seen their king go riding with another man behind him! But the farmer was even more puzzled than they were.

"I still don't know," he said, "which man can be the king."

"You will soon know, my friend," said the king. "Remember that he does not do what others do! Watch carefully. When the others take off their hats to salute him, the king will keep his hat on his head."

Then the king and the farmer got down from the horse and entered the great hall of the palace. The moment they appeared, all of the noblemen and attendants and courtiers took off their hats and saluted the king.

The farmer could not think what to make of it. He and this strange hunter he had rescued in the forest were the only ones in the room with their hats still on their heads. He stood aghast and silent.

"Well," said his companion, "have you found the king now?"

The puzzled farmer shook his head. "I have just one more question, my friend," he said. "Twice I have asked you how I would know the king, and twice I have failed to find him. Now I have only this to say: Tell me, is the king you or me?"

The king laughed heartily at that and told the farmer the truth. Then he thanked the man for his hospitality and for all that he had done. He ordered ten men to accompany the farmer back to his village, and gave him gold and new clothes and the finest mules and donkeys and oxen for his farm.

Thus the hospitable farmer was rewarded by the king, who was as just and generous as every king should be.

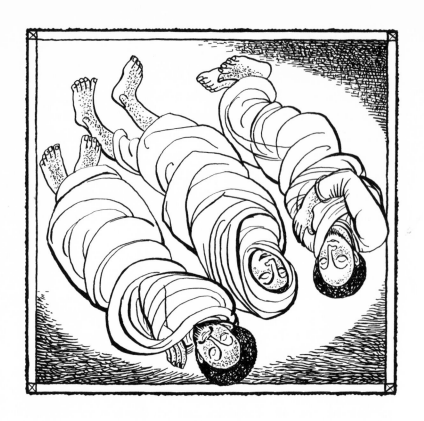

The Three Thieves

Once upon a time there were three thieves who decided to steal enough food to make a good meal. So they stole a goat and some bread, some beer, butter, onions, and salt, and in the evening they took the food to a secret cave.

There they killed the goat and cooked it and made a fine *wat*—a piping hot peppery stew—and put it aside in covered pots, ready to eat the next morning. Then the three thieves lay down and went to sleep.

In the middle of the night one of them woke up. He was hungry, very hungry. He looked at his two friends, still fast asleep. They were snoring and talking to themselves in their dreams. He could not sleep for hunger, so he got up very quietly and went to the place where they had put the food and the beer. He took the lids off the pots and smelled the *wat,* and then he broke off a piece of bread, dipped it in the stew, and began to eat. He ate and ate until he was full, and he drank all the beer. Only a few scraps were left in the bottoms of the pots. After this he lay down again and slept soundly.

When morning came, one of the other two thieves wakened his friends to tell them it was time to eat. They all got up to fetch the food when the thief who had eaten it said to the others: "Haven't you had any dreams, brothers?"

They said they had, and all three sat down to hear each other's dreams. The two thieves who had slept through the night told theirs first.

"I had a thrilling dream," said one of them. "The men from whom I stole the bread were after me to kill me! They were chasing me with spears and knives. They were gaining on me all the time, but at the last moment I escaped! The earth split open in front of me and I dropped down inside."

"It was a horrible night," said the other thief. "The men from whom I stole the goat were chasing me on horseback. I tried to hide from them, but they found me and came riding down on me. At the last moment I escaped by shooting myself like a bullet into the sky."

The thief who had eaten the food listened to his two friends and then he said: "Now you have told your dreams, I expect you will want to hear mine. Well, I dreamed I was lost in a desert and I was very hungry. But I found a whole feast of delicious food—and I ate it."

When his two friends opened the food dishes and found them empty, they knew at once what had happened. They turned on the third thief and shouted at him: "Why did you eat it all alone without waking us?"

He thought for a moment before he replied. "Well," he said, "one of you was down in the earth and the other was shot into the sky. So how could I find you and wake you?"

The Wise Father

Once there was a man who had many sons. When he was old and death was near, he called his sons together. He told them each to bring two sticks. They did as he said.

Then he told each one of them to break one of the sticks. Each son took a stick in his hands and snapped it in two.

When they had done this, the father told them to tie their other sticks together in one bundle. "Now," he said, "break the bundle of sticks."

The eldest son took the bundle and tried to break it on his knee. He failed.

"All of you try to break it," said the father.

They all tried, but they could not break the bundle of sticks.

"Now listen, my children," said the father. "You have learned a good lesson. Each one of you alone is as weak as a single stick. But if you are together, you are strong. Always remember that when slender threads are wound together, they will make a rope to bind a lion."

The Adventurous Mouse

Once there was a mouse who lived with her mother. One day she told her mother that she wanted to go out and see the world, but her mother would not let her go alone.

"The world is much too dangerous," said the mother mouse. "We have many enemies that you know nothing about. You are young and inexperienced. You must wait until you are as old and wise as the rest of us before you go out alone."

But the small mouse would not listen, and one day when her mother was not looking, she ran out to see the world.

31

She walked and walked until she came to the house of a farmer. There in the field beside the house were two of the strangest creatures she had ever seen. One was a friendly and beautiful creature, but the other was so terrible that the little mouse turned tail and ran and never stopped running until she was safely home.

"Oh, mother!" she cried. "I have been out in the world and I've seen such astonishing things!"

"My child," said her mother, "I told you that you must not go out alone. You know nothing about the dangers of the world. What have you seen?"

"I saw two creatures," said the little mouse. "One of them was beautiful. He had four legs and his skin was pure white and smooth. He had a tail that moved from left to right, and a beautiful beard on his chin. He did not frighten me at all, and I would gladly have played with him in the field if I had not seen the other creature—the terrible one! He was red and ugly. He had a very small head with a sort of red topknot on it. He walked on two legs, and he had two wings that he stretched out when he saw me. Oh, I was frightened! I knew how dangerous he was, and I ran just as fast as I could. You see, I do know about the dangers of the world!"

Her mother listened patiently and then she said: "My child, I told you that you are young and inexperienced, but you would not hear me. You are lucky to have come home alive, for you were quite mistaken about the creatures that you saw."

"But how could I be?" said the little mouse. "I saw them with my own eyes."

"My child," said the mother mouse, "you saw them, but you do not know what they are. The two-legged creature with wings, whom you thought so ugly and frightening, is the cock. He is a peaceful and blessed creature. He is not our enemy. But the other one—the one you call beautiful and nice to play with—is our greatest enemy. He chases us everywhere; he wages war against us without mercy. He is the cat!

"Now do you think you know so much about the world?"

The Clever Wizard

Once upon a time, long ago, there lived a rich wizard who was famous throughout the country. Noblemen and officials and great men respected his wisdom and came to seek his advice, while all the people looked up to him as though he were an angel from heaven.

But there was one nobleman who had never liked the wizard. He had long intended to kill him, but he could find no way to do it. Then he thought of a new and cunning plan.

He went to the king and said to him: "Your Majesty, you claim to rule this country and all its people, but the truth is that the people do not look upon you as their king. Instead they obey the commands of an evil wizard. They consider him to be their leader and their prophet. He tells them many lies—even lies about you, O King!—and I greatly fear he is a threat to your throne."

The king was very angry when he heard this. He called ten of his guards and ordered them to bring the wizard to court at once. After the guards had gone, the king told his court attendants to be ready to chop off the head of the wizard as soon as the king gave the signal.

Soon the wizard was captured and dragged before the king. "I have heard," said the king in a loud voice, "that you are a liar and that you have taken money from my people for the false things you tell them. Is that true? Tell me, who are you and what do you do for a living?"

"Your Majesty," replied the wizard, "I am a wise man. I know much about the past and the present. I also tell of the future."

The king listened to the words of the wizard, and then he said: "If you think you are such a wise man, I will ask you one thing. Perhaps you can tell me when I am going to die."

The wizard thought for a while before he answered. "Your Majesty will die—on the next morning after my death."

All the courtiers, who believed in the wizard and his prophecies, turned pale at this saying. The king trembled. He gave no signal to chop off the wizard's head. Instead he ordered his servants at once to look after the wizard and to treat him as the great man he was.

From that day on, the wizard lived at the king's palace. The people loved and revered him more than ever, and the king spared no trouble to give him happiness, riches, and a long, long life.

34

The Quarrel Between the Hyena and the Monkey

Once the hyena and the monkey had a quarrel and went to a judge to settle their differences. But the judge was afraid to pass judgment on their case.

"If I condemn the hyena," he said to himself, "the hyena will eat up all my cattle. And if I condemn the monkey, he will eat up all my corn! So what am I to do?"

The judge thought for a while, and then he told the hyena and the monkey to go to the elders of the village.

He said the case was too difficult for him to judge alone.

So off they went to the elders and told their case again. The elders thought over the matter as the judge had done, and they talked about it among themselves.

"This is very difficult," they said. "If we support the monkey, the hyena will eat our cattle. But if we support the hyena, the monkey will eat our corn."

They were puzzled to know what to do until one of them remembered a poor man who lived nearby. He was so poor that he had nothing to lose—neither cattle nor corn. They quickly told the two animals to go to him and assured them that he was a wise man, who could easily settle their case.

So the hyena and the monkey went to the poor man's little house, and the elders were glad to be rid of them. The poor man was at home, and the animals stated their case once more. He listened to all they had to say and promised to settle their quarrel if he could.

"But first," he said, "I must talk with each of you alone."

They agreed to that, and while the monkey climbed a tree, the poor man took the hyena aside. "Oh, Mr. Hyena," he said, "I wonder how you came to quarrel with this dirty, moth-eaten monkey! He is no companion for you! You are a hero—big and fierce and *very* clever! Therefore it is far better for you to ignore this foolish quarrel and make peace with the monkey. To quarrel with him is unworthy of a hyena. Your people will look down on you. They will scorn you!"

"Why, of course, you are right," said the hyena. "I see my mistake! I have no wish to be scorned and laughed at for the sake of such a small, miserable creature—one beneath my notice! I shall pursue this case no further!"

The hyena drew himself up to his full height and went

off to look for bones in the village rubbish dump, and the man called the monkey down from the tree.

"Oh, Mr. Monkey," he said, "I wonder how you came to quarrel with this dirty, smelly hyena who eats rotten things. As I see you, you are a handsome, elegant creature with the fur of the lion and the courage of the leopard. It is unworthy of you to argue with this dirty hyena. What will your people think of you? Would it not be better to abandon the case and have nothing more to do with hyenas?"

"Ah, yes," said the monkey, "I see what you mean. I scorn to quarrel with such an animal as the hyena! My case against him is finished!"

Then the poor man called the two animals together, and it was like a miracle! They made their peace at once and went their separate ways.

And when the village people heard the story, they smiled and said: "The judge and the elders failed. The rich and powerful ones could do nothing to solve the case, but no one is as determined as a man who is poor."

The King's Questions

Once upon a time a king called together his noblemen and attendants and asked them four questions.

"Who is rich and at the same time a miser?

"Who is generous but old?

"What is the greatest plant on earth?

"What is the greatest animal on earth?"

His people thought and thought and tried their best to solve the riddles, and these were the answers they agreed upon:

"The one who is rich and miserly at the same time is a man who has much wealth but never gives to others.

38

"The one who is generous but old is an old man who gives his money away without a thought for tomorrow, when he will be too old to work for his living.

"The greatest plant on earth is a tall, tall tree, like the *zigba* tree of the mountains.

"The greatest animal on earth is the elephant."

But the king said, "No, no! Your answers are all wrong!" And try as they would, they could not find answers that satisfied him.

News of the king's riddles spread through the land, and many people puzzled over them. After some days a poor man came to the palace gate and asked to see the king. He said he had solved the riddles. When he came before the king, the noblemen and attendants laughed at him. How could he—a poor man in ragged clothes—give the right answers when all of them had failed?

But the king insisted on hearing the poor man's words. And these were his answers to the riddles:

"The One who is rich yet miserly is God. He has the power to do anything and everything, but He does not use His power.

"The one who is generous but old is the Earth. It is old, very old, but it gives us everything it has.

"The greatest plant on earth is the Cotton plant. It is small, but it gives us what we need most of all—clothes to cover our bodies.

"The greatest animal on earth is the Cock. He is not great in size, but he is very great in wisdom; for it is the Cock, every morning, who tells us the time."

Then the king was happy and he said: "Yours are indeed the true answers!"

He praised the poor man before the whole court and gave him such a rich reward that the man was poor no longer.

The Faithful Servant

Once there was a faithful servant who served his master for more than ten years. In those days, long ago, pieces of salt were used as money, and this servant's yearly wage was one bar of salt, known as *amolé*.

Every year, when his master gave him the salt, the servant would dip it in water and say to himself: "If this salt melts away in the water, it means that I have not served my master faithfully. If it does not melt, then it means that I have been a true and faithful servant."

Every year he dipped the salt in water, and every year it melted away. But the servant kept on hoping and hoping that the salt would remain whole, and one year his dream came true. The bar of salt lay in the water, and not a grain of it melted.

The servant took it up with joy and ran to his master. "Oh, master," he said, "please take this salt and use it to buy something for me in the market—anything that comes in your way!"

The master agreed and took the salt. He was a merchant—a very clever man at buying and selling—and he was about to set out for a market in a distant town. He joined a whole caravan of other merchants, bound for the same place, and off they went with their strings of pack-donkeys, loaded with goods for sale.

When at last the merchants reached the town, they had a busy day of trading in the market, and the master forgot all about the servant's salt until he was ready to start for home. By then it was too late to buy anything. The market day was over.

But the master did not want to go home without buying something for his faithful servant. While he was wondering what to do, he remembered what his servant had said. "He asked me to buy anything that came in my way," said the master to himself. "So—anything will do!"

The master looked about him, and there in the road he saw a boy holding a cat. It was a scrawny little cat, and it would be a bad bargain, but the master called the boy and offered him the bar of salt in exchange for the cat. The boy agreed at once and ran off happily with the piece of salt, and the merchant started for home with his string of loaded donkeys—and the cat.

It took the merchant caravan three days and three nights to reach home. On the way they stopped for the night in a forest. They unloaded the tired donkeys, piled up their sacks of grain and bundles of cloth, and made

41

their camp under the trees. But suddenly they heard a strange noise—a rustling, pattering, and squeaking.

The forest was full of rats!

The rats came streaming into the merchants' camp. They swarmed over the bags and the bundles. They gnawed through the sacks and gobbled the grain. They even attacked the rolls of cloth. In vain the merchants rushed up and down. They tried to kill the rats with sticks and knives; they tried to drive them off with shouting. But still the rats came pouring out of the forest until the merchants were in despair.

All except the master of the faithful servant!

His goods were guarded by the cat, the scrawny little cat! She raced up and down, everywhere at once. She pounced on the rats like a leopard until the ground was littered with their bodies, and the rest of them turned tail and fled with squeals of terror.

When the other merchants saw what the cat could do, they came running to their friend and begged him to let them hire the cat to guard *their* goods from the rats.

So the master let them hire the cat, each in his turn. She worked the whole night through to guard the merchants' goods, and by the next morning she had earned the master much money. He let her ride proudly on his leading pack-donkey and sleep to her heart's content.

At the end of the third day the master arrived home, and the faithful servant ran out to welcome him and to see what he had bought with the slab of salt. But all the master had for him was the scrawny little cat!

The poor servant did not know what to say, but the master gave him no chance to speak. He told the servant about the rats in the forest and the wonderful deeds of the little cat, and he offered to buy the cat to be a protector of the merchant caravans.

So the faithful servant agreed to sell the cat, and his grateful master gave him so much money that the servant was a rich man to the end of his days.

And that is why people say, from that day to this: "Faithfulness is wealth."

The Divided Students

Four students were walking home when suddenly they saw a big piece of bread lying in the road.

They all ran to pick it up. They bumped into each other and rolled on the ground, grabbing at the bread. Each of them tried to get it for himself. They struggled and argued fiercely.

One of them tried to settle the dispute by telling the others he was the oldest. He would take charge of the bread and divide it equally among them all. But the others refused to listen and went on arguing.

Presently a priest passed by and asked them what was the trouble. They told him, and of course each student claimed to have found the bread first.

The priest said, "Give the bread to me. I will divide it into four pieces and give you your fair shares."

The students agreed. The priest took the bread and divided it into four parts. Then he put the pieces of bread in a row and showed each student his share. They stretched out their hands to take the bread, but the priest stopped them.

"Oh, no," said he. "Wait until I am sure that all the pieces are exactly equal in size."

"You are right, Father," said one of the students. "My share is the smallest."

"Of course," said the priest, "your share is indeed the smallest. But this one is the biggest." And he ate a mouthful of the biggest piece of bread.

"Do not worry, my children, all your shares will soon be equal. Now here is one that is still too big!" And he took another piece and ate almost half of it.

"Alas!" cried one of the students. "That was my piece and it was the right size. Why do you take half of it?"

"Do not worry, my child," said the priest. "I will make the others equal to yours." And he ate a mouthful of each of the other three pieces.

But still they were not equal.

"Just a bite here and a bite there, and all will be well!" said he.

The students watched him in bewildered silence until the priest swallowed the last mouthful of bread and left them standing in the road.

They looked into each other's eyes, and at last the oldest student said: "I told you I would divide the bread fairly among us. You would not listen to me. Therefore we have lost everything we had."

They remembered the words of the old saying: "United we stand; divided we fall." And they went sadly on their way with equal shares—of nothing at all.

The Meeting of the Young Mice

Once upon a time all the young mice in the town held a
meeting. It was a meeting of protest against the power of
the cat. Something had to be done, for the cat was the
terror of the town.

The subject of their discussion was "How to kill the
cat," but they quickly agreed that the cat was far too big
and strong for any mouse to kill. Then one young mouse
had a wonderful idea and rose up to tell the others.

The cat was quiet and stealthy in his attacks, but
suppose they hung a bell around his neck! Then they
would always hear him coming and be able to run to

safety! And the cat, unable to catch any mice, would soon starve to death! Every young mouse at the meeting squeaked with joy. All their problems were solved.

But there was one old mouse among them, who had been sitting quietly in a corner, listening to everything that went on. When the young mice had finished their meeting and were about to go home, the old one wanted to speak.

"I have a question," he called out over the chatter of the others.

But the young mice would not listen. "You old mice are always doubtful and cowardly and full of objections," they said. "We have just solved the biggest problem of all mice. Do you want to object to this noble idea?"

"Wait!" said the old mouse. "You young ones are always in a hurry to do something, whether you know how to do it or not. Now let me ask you one question: Who among you will go to the sleeping cat and hang the bell around his neck?"

The young mice looked at each other, and suddenly not one of them had a word to say. Not one of them moved a whisker to volunteer for the task of putting the bell on the cat. The meeting broke up very quietly, and the old mouse smiled to himself as he trotted home.

"To think and to act are two very different things," he said, "and old heads are often wiser in their thinking than young ones."

The Coward and His Luck

In a small country there reigned a rich king who was very disappointed in his son. The young prince was a coward. Many times his father had tried to make him brave, but it was no use. The prince would run away from a fight or a hunt, and always, when he was frightened, he would cry and weep like a little child. His father was in despair.

One day the prince went out alone to the forest. When he wanted to return to the palace, it was dark. He dared not go home for fear of meeting wild animals, so he decided to climb a tree and spend the night there.

While he was looking for a tree to climb, he saw five

thieves sharing the meat of an ox they had stolen. The prince was hungry and he begged them to give him some meat. But all they would give him was the skin. He took it sadly and hauled it up a tree. Then he settled himself on a branch and fell asleep, with the skin wrapped warmly around him.

At midnight a hungry hyena came that way, sniffing the good smell of the skin. The hyena stopped under the tree and gazed up at the man. When the prince heard the voice of the hyena beneath him, he woke in terror. He was so frightened he fell off the branch right on top of the hyena. He grabbed the animal by the tail, and the hyena was so frightened he ran off at top speed, dragging the man behind him.

On and on he ran until at dawn they reached a town, and there the hyena suddenly stopped. His heart burst within him and he fell down dead.

The poor prince was even more frightened than before. All he could do was cry and weep, still holding the dead hyena by the tail. People came running out of their houses and laughed at him.

Now the king of that town had a beautiful daughter, and when she heard news of the young man and the hyena she sent messengers to bring the stranger to the palace. As soon as she saw him, she fell in love with him. She loved his handsome face, but she did not like the way he cried and wept.

"The king my father likes brave men," she said, "so when he asks you why you cry and weep, tell him that this is the custom of heroes in your country."

The prince was summoned by the king and answered the question as the princess had told him to, but the king was suspicious. He wanted the stranger to prove he was really a hero. So the king ordered the young man to go forth and hunt a mighty lion that had been terrifying the country for a long time.

"But you must show me the lion," the king warned him. "Do not come here and *tell* me you have slain the lion! Bring it back and let me see it—alive or dead!"

The prince began to shiver and shake. He opened his mouth to say he could not possibly kill the lion, but the princess signaled to him to keep quiet. She then told the king that the young man was known to be a great lion hunter.

Before the prince set out to find the lion, the princess gave him a long drink of *tej,* the powerful honey drink that can make a man feel braver and stronger than ever before. She even gave his horse some *tej* and tied a bottle of it to the saddle. Then she told the young man to go. Away he went with the speed of the wind, feeling dizzy and drunk and marvelously brave.

By the time he reached the forest where the lion lived, the prince was growing sleepy, and his horse was very tired and could run no longer.

They stopped under a tree, and the prince got down from the horse and took off the saddle. He forgot about the bottle tied to the saddlebow. He dropped the saddle heavily on the ground. The bottle was broken and the precious *tej* all spilt, but the prince was too sleepy to care. He and his horse lay down under the tree and were soon fast asleep.

Now the tree was near the lion's cave, and presently the lion came out. Seeing the man and the horse, he stepped toward them. They lay so still he thought they were dead. Then he saw and smelt the pool of *tej,* and as he was thirsty, he began to drink. He liked the taste, and he drank up all the *tej.* Suddenly his legs began to sway and would not hold him up! The lion was drunk.

When he tried to walk, he fell over the sleeping man. The prince awoke, and in his fright he caught the lion by the hair of the mane. He lay across the back of the lion and held on tight. The lion was so surprised he jumped up and began to stagger through the forest with the man on his back. Faster and faster went the lion, trying to shake off the man, but still the prince held on. He had never meant to do it, but he was riding the lion!

Soon the forest was behind them and they were galloping into the town. The people rushed after them, shouting and screaming. The lion was surrounded by hundreds of people, and suddenly he stopped dead—right under the windows of the king's palace. The prince still clung to his mane and began to cry and weep, but this time nobody laughed at him. Everyone believed it was the custom of heroes in his country to cry and weep after doing a brave deed, and they began to praise the young man for capturing the terrible lion and riding him home. Who else, they cried, would have the courage to ride a lion?

The king was watching all this from his window. Now he sent soldiers to seize and bind the lion and servants to bring the young man into the hall of the palace. The king too had words of praise for the rider of the lion, and then he gave the prince his daughter's hand in marriage.

So the coward was married to the beautiful princess, and the fame of his courage spread throughout the land. When the old king died, the prince became king, ruling wisely and well, and all his people loved him.

The Man and His Daughter

There was a man who had many children. The eldest was a boy and the second was a girl. The man liked his eldest son better than any of the other children. He brought him up in comfort and showed him love and tenderness. He did not care so much for his daughter.

When the boy and the girl were old enough for marriage, their father arranged for their weddings and prepared a good wedding ceremony. The daughter was married to a hard-working man who was neither very rich nor very poor. She lived happily with her husband, but the favorite son soon divorced his wife. He went off to live in another village where he became chief treasurer to a wealthy man.

The father had many younger children, and another child was soon to be born. The family was always in need of more food and more clothes, and the man became so poor trying to feed and clothe them all that he did not know what to do.

At last his wife advised him to go to their eldest son, who had grown very rich. So the man set out and walked for two days to reach the house of his son. He told the servants who he was, but the son was so busy that he had no time just then to meet his father. He kept the poor man standing outside the gate all day.

At last the servants let the father in. He met his son and told him he had come seeking help.

"I can't help you!" said the son angrily. "I haven't the money to pay the wages of my own servants, so how can I give you anything?"

And without another word he left the father standing there and sat down to his work in another room.

The father went sadly home and told his wife the whole story. They had nothing to eat, and the whole family suffered. At last the man decided to go to his daughter, although he knew that her husband was not very rich. Even a little help would be better than nothing.

It was a long walk to the daughter's house, and he came to her gate very weary and covered with dust. But as soon as the daughter saw him, she rejoiced and welcomed him in. She killed a sheep, and there was a great feast. She told all her neighbors that this was her father whom she had not seen for years. He stayed in her house for three days, and then she sent him home with a bag of money, a fine mule, and a bundle of new clothes for her mother and small brothers and sisters.

Riding his new mule, the father soon reached his village. Before he came to his house he met one of the neighbors who was amazed to see him dressed in new clothes and a new hat and riding on a mule. The neighbor asked him where he had found such wealth and the man answered that it was all a gift from his daughter.

"Congratulations!" said another neighbor. "Your wife had a baby this morning."

"Is it a boy or a girl?" cried the father.

"Good news for you!" said the neighbor with joy. "It is a son!"

"A son? Then I will never go back to my house!" said the man in disgust, and he swung his mule around to ride away.

But all the neighbors came out and begged him to stay. "God has given you this child," they cried. "You cannot fight against God!"

So the man consented to go home to his house. He gave his wife all that their daughter had given him. The whole family had food to eat and clothes to wear, and their hearts were glad and grateful for the gifts of the generous daughter.

The Two Thieves

Once there lived two thieves who used to work together and share their loot.

One day they were hiding on the edge of the forest, watching for people coming home from a village market with the things they had bought. Soon the thieves saw a man coming toward them. On his back he carried a *silicha,* a big leather bag, and he was leading a fine sheep on the end of a rope.

The moment the thieves saw him, they planned a trick to take away his goods. One of them hid himself in the forest; the other ran a little farther on and lay down in the middle of the path. The man soon reached the spot where the thief was lying, and he was about to pass him by when the thief cried out: "O dear traveler, I am blind and I don't know where I am. Please, in God's name, lead me to the next village!"

The man felt sorry for him. "I would be pleased to help you, my friend," he said. "But how can I do it? I am carrying this great bag of honey on my back and leading a sheep behind me!"

The thief thought for a moment and then he said: "If you will hold my right hand and lead me along, I will hold the rope in my left hand and lead your sheep."

The man agreed, and off they went, with the thief leading the sheep. After a mile or two the other thief, who was hiding in the forest, crept up behind them, untied the rope, and took away the sheep.

A little later the thief who was pretending to be blind said to the man who was leading him: "It's a strange thing, my friend, but this rope that I am holding has suddenly become very light!"

The man stopped and turned round. The sheep was gone! He was angry. He thought the sheep had slipped out of its rope and got left behind, and he decided to run back and look for it. He put the heavy bag of honey into the hands of the thief and told him to wait there until the sheep was found.

The man hurried away down the path, and he had no sooner disappeared than the thief ran off with the bag of honey and joined his friend in the forest.

Thus the poor man who had trusted the thief lost everything he had bought at the market—both sheep and honey.

He learned too late the truth of the old saying: "He who does not doubt will come to ruin."

Billicho and the Cannibal

Billicho was a clever boy. He was admired by all the people in his village, except the boys who looked after the cattle. Billicho was a herder of cattle too, and the other boys did not like him because he was cleverer than all the rest of them. They thought his cunning and his tricks were evil, and one day they plotted to kill him.

They told Billicho they had found gold and diamonds hidden in a hole in the hillside. "But the hole is too narrow for us to go in," they said. "You are small, and you can go down and get the gold and jewels."

Billicho believed what they said, and he crawled into

the hole they showed him. As soon as he was inside, the boys blocked the entrance so that he could not get out.

Billicho knew he was trapped, but he was not afraid. He crawled on and found himself in a big cave. Still he went on and on, following the wall of the cave, until a narrow passage led him out to the open air again on the far side of the hill. He was in a big green garden, but the garden was owned by Chirak, a terrible cannibal.

The cannibal was a woman, huge and fierce and ugly. She seized hold of Billicho and tied him hand and foot. Then she told her daughter to boil water in the big pot.

"And when the water is hot," she said, "untie his foot and tell him to dip his toes in the water to make sure it has boiled. Then throw him into the pot and cook him."

While the mother cannibal went to a neighbor to borrow a knife, the daughter untied Billicho's foot and told him to see if the water had boiled. Billicho answered that he could not possibly test the water by putting his foot in it. "My feet are as hard as a dried oxhide," he said. "I can only feel the heat of the water with my arms. Untie my hands and I can tell you whether the water has boiled."

She untied his hands and got ready to throw him into the pot. But Billicho was clever. He bent down and pretended to test the water in the pot, and when the daughter tried to push him in, he jumped aside and pushed her instead. She fell headfirst into the boiling water, and Billicho fled.

He ran through the cannibal's garden and out through the gate in the fence. He ran up the hill and over the hilltop, and he did not stop running till he came to his village on the other side.

The village boys were aghast to see him, safe and well. They knew then that they were no match for Billicho, and they never tried to trick him again.

The Man and the Snake

A monkey, a rat, a snake, and a man were traveling to a far-off country, and when darkness came, they asked a rich man to let them sleep at his house for one night.

The man agreed, but he would not allow the snake to sleep in the house. "The others can come in," said he, "but you, O Snake, cannot live at peace with any other creature. You are the enemy of all. So you must stay out."

But the snake begged to be let in. "Do you think I am more cruel than Man?" the snake said. "Please trust me and let me in!"

The rich man at last took pity on him and let him pass

the night in the house with the others. In the morning they all thanked the man and went on their journey.

After many years the rich man became very poor. He had nothing to eat, not even a handful of flour or a scrap of meat for the *wat* pot. He thought of the four friends—the rat, the man, the monkey, and the snake—who had slept the night in his house. He decided to find them and to ask them for help.

First he found the rat and told her of his misfortune. The rat hurried away at once to a rich man's house and stole a box half full of gold. She brought the gold to her friend to help him in his need. He thanked her with all his heart and then went to find the man.

He told the man about his poverty and showed him the gold, the gift of the rat. But the man felt no pity. Instead he beat the visitor, took away the box of gold, and threw him into a deep pit.

The poor man who had once been rich was in despair. He lay in the bottom of the pit, a helpless prisoner, when suddenly his friend the monkey appeared.

"Why, how did you come to be here, my good friend?" asked the monkey, and the poor man told him all that had happened. The monkey at once took the man on his back and climbed with him up the side of the pit.

The man was now so bruised and weary he could hardly stand. It was all he could do to drag himself to his friend the snake and tell again the tale of his misfortunes. When the snake heard how the poor man had been beaten and robbed, he said: "I told you once, my friend, that Man is cruel. You would not believe me then. Do you see now that my words were true, and that Man is indeed the most evil creature on the earth? Are you ready to do as I say? Man has made you suffer grievous things, but if you listen to me, I can help you grow rich again."

"What must I do, my good friend?" asked the man.

"Not far from here," said the snake, "there lives a wealthy landowner who has an only daughter. She is to be married in three days' time. I shall go today and bite her, and she will become very ill." And then the snake explained what the man must do.

The next day everyone in the house of the landowner was stricken with grief. The daughter had been bitten by a snake. She was so ill that already she seemed near to death. Wise men were called in, but no one could help her. Her father was in despair.

Then a stranger came to the gate and said he was skilled in curing snakebites. The servants took him at once to the girl's father.

"I have a cure that never fails," the stranger said, just as the snake had told him to say. "But before I use my skill, I would ask you to grant me one thing."

"I will give you anything!" cried the father, though he did not believe for a moment that the poor, ragged stranger could heal the girl.

"Will you promise me your daughter's hand in marriage?" asked the man.

"Yes, yes, anything you desire!" said the father. "If only you can cure my child!"

He hurried the man into the room where the daughter was lying. She lay quite still, with her eyes closed, as though she were dead. The poor man had never seen anyone so beautiful. He knelt down beside her bed and took out the leaf of a tree the snake had shown him. He touched the leaf to the bite on the girl's foot. At once the marks of the bite vanished and the foot was no longer swollen. The girl opened her eyes and sat up, completely cured and more beautiful than ever.

The father kept his promise. Three days later, with

great rejoicing, the girl was married to the man who had saved her life, and because of the kindness of the snake, the man lived in wealth and happiness with his beautiful wife.

An Act of Kindness

An old man was dying when he called his three sons and divided his wealth among them equally. Then he held out a jewel that sparkled in his hand.

"I will give this jewel," he said, "to any one of you who has done an act of kindness."

The eldest son spoke first. "Once a man left much money with me, trusting me to keep it for him until he returned from a far-off journey. I kept the money, and when he came back I gave him all he had left with me, taking none of it for myself. The man wanted to pay me for what I had done, but I would take nothing. Isn't this an act of kindness?"

The old man replied, "No, my son. This is honesty; it is not an act of kindness."

Then the second son began to speak. "Once I was passing a pond," he said, "and I saw a child drowning in the water. I did not care about my own life. I jumped into the water and saved the child and carried him to his mother. She was very happy and grateful to me. Isn't this an act of kindness, Father?"

"No, my son," the father answered. "You did well, but that was sympathy, not an act of kindness."

Finally the youngest son spoke. "I was walking near a gorge one night," he said, "and I saw my enemy lying on the clifftop at the edge of the gorge. He was drunk and sound asleep. I could see that if he moved in his sleep he would fall into the gorge and be killed. So I went quietly and taking him by both hands, I pulled him to a safe place. Isn't that kindness?"

The old man was very pleased. "Yes," he said, kissing the cheeks of his youngest son. "There is no better act of kindness than doing good to an enemy." And he gave the jewel to the youngest son.

Too Much Praise

A man who lived in a big village married a girl from the country. She had never lived in a village before. Her husband had to teach her how to behave and what to do in his house.

"Your most important work is to keep everything clean," he told her. "I want all the clothes and pots and pans to be spotlessly clean."

She promised to do everything he commanded.

The next day she washed all the plates and the clothes. She also cleaned the room. Her husband was very pleased. "You are taking my advice, my dear," he said. "I am very happy with what you have done. This is a fine beginning."

All the neighbors admired her. "What a wonderful woman!" they said.

The girl was very happy.

On the third day she rose from her bed early in the morning and cleaned everything she could lay hands on. She washed the clothes, the floor, the chairs, and the table. Everything in the house was clean. Her husband saw this and praised her. "You are becoming the most careful, tidy, and hard-working woman in our village," he told her.

He also told his neighbors about the remarkable things his wife had done. All the neighbors admired her more than ever.

On the fourth day she looked around the house for dirty things to wash. But she could find none. Then suddenly she saw a grimy old book in a worn cover lying in a box. "How dirty that looks!" she said. "My husband will praise me if I clean it for him. He will think no woman exists but me!"

So she took the book and washed it, over and over again, scrubbing each parchment page, and at last she hung up the book to dry in the sun.

When the husband came home that day the first thing he saw was his book, hanging out to dry. The pages were scrubbed so clean that the writing and pictures were nearly all scrubbed away. At first he was angry and began to shout at his wife, but then he stopped his angry words.

"It is not your fault," he said. "If I had not praised you so much, you would not have washed my book."

And ever afterward the people remembered the danger of too much praise, and there was a saying in that village: "When she was praised too much, she washed a book!"

The Clever Temari

A *temari* is a student who is training to be a priest or a village teacher. With a sheepskin about his shoulders and a staff in his hand, he wanders along the roads and footpaths of the highlands, stopping at the ancient monasteries to study with learned monks. He has nothing to call his own and he must beg for food and shelter in the villages on his way.

Temaris are the heroes of many, many tales. Everywhere the temaris wander, people tell stories about their sharp wits, their jokes, and above all, their cleverness. A clever temari is a match for anyone, even a king. . . .

It is said that long ago in the city of Gondar there reigned a king who hated thieves. If a man were charged with robbery in the kingdom, there was no question about his fate. He was put to death at once.

One day the king decided to make sure that there was not a single thief left in the city. So he ordered his servants to leave a sheep wandering about the streets with no shepherd. About the neck of the sheep they hung a knife.

The sheep roamed about all day and came quietly home to the palace in the evening. This went on for several days until a hungry temari found the sheep in a field. He caught the animal and killed it with the knife.

When the sheep did not come home that night, the king was sure it had been stolen, and he suspected that the thief was a temari. There were a great many temaris in Gondar, and he ordered them all to assemble next day in the hall of the palace.

In the morning, the king commanded his servants to drop a few pieces of gold in the courtyard outside the hall. He thought the thief who had stolen the sheep would surely see the gold and want to steal that too. He would bend down to pick it up and give himself away!

The king then took his place in a tower with a small window overlooking the courtyard. There he could watch for the thief without being seen.

The temaris came pouring in through the palace gate in their ragged clothes and sheepskin cloaks. The king watched them walk in a procession to the great hall. Not one of them bent down to pick up the gold. Yet when they had passed, the gold was gone!

The temari who had stolen the sheep had been waiting at the palace gate since early morning. He had seen the servants dropping the gold. He had rubbed wax under his shoes, just enough to make them sticky. Then he walked solemnly into the palace hall and out again with the gold firmly stuck to the soles of his feet!

The king was very angry. He was determined to catch the thief and get rid of him.

A few days later he arranged a *gibir,* a royal feast, and invited all the temaris to come. The finest raw meat and wine were to be served. The king ordered his servants to give the temaris as much wine as they would drink, and he set spies to watch them and listen to all they said.

The guests were assembled. The wine was poured, and very soon the temaris were drunk. They began to talk and laugh and sing, and the one who had stolen the sheep and gold was the greatest talker of them all. He began to boast, telling his friends exactly what he had done.

But one of the king's spies was listening. The spy had drunk no wine, and his eyes and ears were sharp. He kept a close watch on the thief until at last the time came when all the temaris were stretched out on the floor, fast asleep.

Then the spy crept up to the thief and made a mark on his arm, following the king's orders. With the help of that mark, the thief would be caught in the morning. The spy told the king that all was ready, and the king smiled in triumph. This time the thief had no chance of escape! When the temaris left the palace in the morning, each one was to show his arm to the king's servants.

But the thieving temari was awake before the rest and saw the strange mark on his arm. In spite of all the wine he had drunk, he still had his wits about him. He knew what he must do while his friends were still asleep.

When the servants inspected the temaris next morning, every single one of them had the same mark on his arm! They all went streaming out of the palace in a great procession, with the clever temari in their midst. Once more he had outwitted the king!

The Puzzle

Once there lived a girl called Tsehaynesh. Her father was a rich man. She was very beautiful, and every man in the village was attracted by Tsehaynesh.

One day she fell into the river. On the river bank were three men. All three of them had wanted to take her hand in marriage, but her father would not consent. The three men saw Tsehaynesh struggling in the water, and they saw a crocodile take hold of her and drag her by the leg toward the other bank. What could they do?

One of the men was a harp player, and he could not do anything but make music.

68

So he took up his instrument, raised his voice, and sang a verse of poetry.

> "Oh, Beauty, come back,
> Do not go away with the crocodile!
> My heart needs you,
> I cannot live without you—
> Come back, my dear, come back!"

When the crocodile heard this, he was so deeply touched by the music and the poetry that he left the girl and turned to listen. Then the second man, who was a hunter, fired his gun and killed the crocodile. The girl was beginning to sink when the third man, who was a good swimmer, jumped into the water. He swam to her side and pulled her safely to the bank.

Thus Tsehaynesh was saved. Her father said he would give her to one of the three men. All three claimed her hand in marriage because of what they had done. Which one of the three men deserved to marry Tsehaynesh?

The Farmer and the Merchant

In Magdala, the capital of Ethiopia in the days of the great Emperor Theodore, there lived a rich merchant. He was well known as a hard and greedy man, not always honest in his dealings with others.

One day he loaded up his donkeys with bags of salt and set out on the long journey from Magdala to the city of Gondar. After a while he stopped by a stream to rest and to drink the pure water.

He did not allow himself to rest for long and was soon on the road again. But as he traveled on with his loaded donkeys, he suddenly stopped in alarm. He had lost a hundred dollars! The money had been tied up in a small bag, and now the bag was gone! He searched for it everywhere, but it was not to be found. All he could do was go back to the stream and look for the money there.

When he reached the stream, he saw a poor farmer sitting on the grassy bank in the exact place where he himself had rested. The farmer was tired and dusty from a long journey, and he too had come to the stream to drink the water.

The merchant asked him if he had found anything lost. The farmer, innocent as he was, said he had found a hundred dollars wrapped in a small bag. "If it happens to be yours, take it," said the farmer, holding out the bag to the merchant.

But the merchant thought for a moment, and within that short time he made a wicked plan. He said: "No, my friend. It was not a hundred dollars only; it was two hundred dollars that I lost."

The farmer denied this. "I only found a hundred dollars," he said.

The merchant refused to accept the farmer's word. He said he would take the farmer before a judge. The poor man agreed to go to court at Magdala, and so, after journeying together to the city, they found themselves at the court of the Emperor Theodore.

In the Emperor's presence they stated their case. As there were no witnesses the dispute was difficult to judge, but the Emperor was wise. He had heard many times of the merchant's greedy and wicked deeds. He knew that the farmer was innocent and the merchant treacherous.

So the Emperor prepared to make his final judgment. "How much did you lose?" he asked the merchant.

"Two hundred dollars, Your Majesty," the merchant answered.

"Well," said the Emperor, "the farmer says he found only one hundred dollars, which of course cannot be yours. Therefore you must seek someone who has found two hundred."

The Emperor then turned to the trembling farmer. "And you," he said, "how much was it that you found?"

"One hundred dollars only, Your Majesty," said the farmer.

"I see there is no one here who has lost a hundred dollars," said the Emperor, "so until someone comes lawfully to claim the money I grant that you may take the hundred dollars for yourself."

Thus the poor farmer took the money that he had found, and the wicked merchant lost what had been his. He learned at bitter cost the truth of the old saying: "One who wishes to take what belongs to another loses what he has."

Sinziro

There was a woman who had seven sons, and all of them were foolish. The woman was unhappy to have such stupid sons.

Then she had an eighth child. He was very short and small. His height was no more than the distance between a man's thumb and middle finger, when the hand is spread. This measure is called a *sinzir;* so the woman called her little son Sinziro. She liked Sinziro because he was very clever. He could outwit any of his neighbors.

One day Sinziro and his brothers set out to steal an ox. When they reached a rich man's farm, the seven brothers told Sinziro to go into the compound and bring out the ox. "You are small," they said, "and no one will notice you."

So Sinziro went inside the compound and came out with the ox. The brothers took the ox away and slaughtered it in the forest, but the seven stupid ones would give no meat to Sinziro. "Let your mother give you meat," they said. "She likes you better than any of us."

Sinziro was very angry at this, and he thought of a trick to play on his brothers. He asked them to give him the bladder of the ox, and since they did not need it for anything, they let him have it.

Sinziro blew into the bladder and filled it full of air. Then he took a stick and climbed a tree and hid himself among the branches. He began to beat with the stick on the blown-up bladder so that it sounded like the footfalls of a person running, and then he cried out at the top of his voice: "I didn't steal the ox by myself! Don't blame me for stealing the ox! My brothers are the thieves—they stole the ox!"

When the foolish brothers heard Sinziro's cries and the thud of the beaten bladder, they thought the owner of the ox was running after them. So they left the meat and ran for their lives.

As soon as they were gone, Sinziro climbed down from the tree and ate all the meat he wanted. A donkey was grazing nearby, and Sinziro loaded the rest of the meat onto its back and trotted home with the donkey, to give the meat to his mother.

When his brothers understood how he had fooled them, they were so angry they burned down his house. All that was left was a heap of ashes. Sinziro said nothing. He simply loaded the ashes onto the backs of ten donkeys and started out on a journey.

He traveled all day with his ten donkeys, and when darkness came, he stopped at a rich man's house and asked if he might spend the night there. The rich man welcomed him in.

Sinziro had a plan. In the morning he went outside to load up the ten donkeys and began at once to wail and cry. "Oh, my flour, my flour! Where is my flour?"

The rich man ran outside and asked him what had happened.

"I had ten loads of flour when I came here last night," cried Sinziro, with the tears running down his cheeks. "Now I see ten loads of ashes! Someone has stolen my flour in the night and left ashes instead!"

He went on crying and cursing until all the neighbors gathered to listen. When the rich man saw the crowd in front of his house, he was afraid of being accused of robbery. His reputation would be ruined. So he gave Sinziro ten loads of flour to replace the ashes and sent him on his way.

Sinziro journeyed home with his flour, and of course his foolish brothers asked him how he had got it. He said he had exchanged the flour for the ashes of his burnt house. The seven brothers at once decided to do the same. They burned down their houses and went to market with bags of ashes. But everyone in the market laughed at them.

Then the brothers knew that Sinziro had fooled them again, and they decided to get rid of him forever. They bound him to a log of wood and threw him into the sea, with no food but a little bagful of peas.

While Sinziro was floating away on the log, a rich man was walking on the shore. He saw the log with the boy on top of it and ordered his servants to haul the log out of the water.

So Sinziro was rescued. The servants set him free, and he stood before the rich man, holding the little bag of peas. The man was amazed by Sinziro's smallness. He asked him who he was and where he came from and why he was floating in the sea.

"I am a messenger from God!" cried Sinziro in a loud voice. "Behold! I have come from heaven to give you this bag! If you open it after one month has passed—neither sooner nor later—you will find gold within. Take the bag and give me some money and a horse so that I may go back whence I came!"

The rich man was very happy. He took the bag of peas, with thanks to God, and gave Sinziro thirty dollars and a good horse.

When Sinziro arrived home, riding the handsome horse, his seven brothers were amazed and angry and ready to kill him. But Sinziro tossed the money to them, and they all began to struggle for a share. Some got hold of the money, and some had none. They were so busy fighting each other that they forgot about Sinziro.

From that day on, the seven stupid brothers never stopped quarreling. This was good for Sinziro, for they had no time to quarrel with him, and at last he could live in peace.

The Three Wise Men

In olden days there lived three wise men who were always reading and pondering over their books. They went to the king and told him how wise they were. They said they had studied everything under heaven, and they wanted the king's permission to travel anywhere and to do whatever they pleased. The king gladly gave them leave to go where they wished. So they went on a journey to a far-off country.

On the way the three wise men came across a dead lion. One of them said: "Let us give life to this lion." And they all agreed that this would be a good thing to do.

"I will fasten his bones to his flesh," said the first wise man.

"I will make him breathe," said the second.

"I will make him move," said the third.

While they were talking, a man was watching them and listening to their words. "Gentlemen," he said, when they had spoken, "you think you are very wise. You want to give life to this beast. But don't you see that he will eat you all?"

The wise men became angry at this. "You are the biggest fool we have ever seen in our lives," they said. "How could we be eaten by the lion whom we have brought to life? You are stupid and know nothing at all. Be off! Go away!"

But the man was not convinced. "It may be as you think," he said. "But let me climb up this tree and see what will happen."

So he climbed up the tree and watched. The three wise men did as they had planned. The first one fastened together the lion's bones and flesh; the second one gave him breath; and the third one made him move.

Then the lion rose up hungrily, and with a mighty roar he pounced on them and ate them—one, two, three.

The man in the tree saw all that happened. He waited until the full-fed lion had gone away before he climbed down from his tree, and as he continued his journey, he said to himself: "When a knife is too sharp, it cuts its own case; when a man has too much wisdom, it leads him to his death."

Two Tales of Aleka Gebrehanna

Aleka Gebrehanna lived in Gondar about eighty years ago. Many tales were told about him, and people still chuckle over them today.

"Aleka," meaning "head" or "chief," is one of the titles given to priests, and Aleka Gebrehanna was a priest, a man of learning, and a poet. He was well known to the Emperor Menelik, who ruled Ethiopia in those days and founded the city of Addis Ababa.

But Aleka was most famous for his quick wits and clever sayings, and the stories often tell how people tried in vain to outwit him.

79

NO HIDES IN THE CHURCH!

Aleka was serving as a priest in one of the churches of Gondar. It was the time of an important festival when all the priests were to join in a great procession and dance and sing to the pounding of drums. Every priest in the procession must wear a white turban and wrap himself in a *shamma* of the finest white cotton. But Aleka's clothes were worn out, and he could not afford to buy a new *shamma*. So he bought a hide in the market and wrapped himself in that.

When he joined the other priests in the procession, they were very upset. Aleka's hide had a terrible smell, and the oil he had put on it stained their beautiful white *shammas* when he rubbed against them in the dance. The priests were so angry that they gathered together afterward and made a law that no hides should be allowed in the church.

The next morning, when Aleka came to the church, still wrapped in the hide, they turned him back at the door. "Go away!" they said. "We have a new law. No hides allowed in the church!"

"I understand," said Aleka. "If this is the new law, it must be obeyed!"

And he ran at once to the room where the church treasures were stored and began to throw out the leather drums and the great hand-written books with their beautiful pictures.

The priests looked on in dismay. "What are you doing?" they cried. "Why are you throwing out the treasures of the church?"

"I am obeying your new law," said Aleka.

He held up a mighty book, written on parchment and bound in leather. "Was this not made from the hides of animals?" he demanded. "In keeping such things in the church you are breaking your new law! If no hides are allowed in the church, no hides will there be!"

I DON'T LIKE FISH

One day a husband and wife had just sat down to a good meal of fish when they saw Aleka coming to their house. Not wanting to share their meal with him, they quickly hid the fish in another room and waited for Aleka to come in. They exchanged greetings in a friendly way and started to talk. But Aleka knew what the man and wife were hiding. He had smelled the fish the moment he entered the house, and he was hungry.

Presently he began to talk about food. "This morning I went to a friend's house," he said, "and he invited me to eat with him."

"What happened then?" asked the man, curious to know whether he had eaten.

"Of course I did not eat," said Aleka. "The meal was fish, and I don't like fish."

The husband and wife looked at each other. The smell of the fish was making them very hungry, and they were no longer afraid of having to share their meal with Aleka.

"How unfortunate," said the husband, "that you don't like fish. We have a meal of fish ready now, and we would have liked you to enjoy it too. We are so sorry you cannot eat with us!"

Aleka looked intently at the fish as they brought it out and sat down to eat. Then he came over to join them.

"You have no need to be sorry," he said. "I see that this is a fine, large fish. I like this kind! What I don't like are the little fishes, full of bones and prickles!"

And so saying, he sat down with them and ate such a full share of the fish that the husband and wife got little more than the bones and the tail.

The Hair of the Lion

A husband and wife lived in a certain village in Tigré. The husband was never happy. He was always late coming home from his work, and sometimes he spent a whole night away. His wife was worried. She was angry every time he came in late, and she insulted him with harsh words. But this did not make him any better.

So one day the woman went to the wise old man who had been witness to their wedding, and she asked him to arrange for a divorce.

"My husband does not come home regularly, and he will not eat my cooking. I do not want him any more!"

83

The wise old man listened to her bitter words, and then he said: "I have heard your problem. But you must not think of divorce. I know a far better way for you. There is a medicine that can make your husband a different man. He will be glad to come home and to be obedient to you in everything."

The woman was very pleased to hear this and wanted to get hold of the medicine at once.

"That," said the old man, "is not easy. To prepare the medicine I must get a single hair of a living lion. Can you bring me that single hair of a lion?"

The woman thought for a moment and then she said: "Yes, I am ready to bring it."

The old man was surprised, but he said nothing. He knew now how much she loved her husband.

The next morning he showed the woman the river where the lion was often seen coming to drink, and he left her there with a servant and a bag of fresh meat.

The woman stayed hidden behind some bushes until the lion came down to the river and drank. At first the woman was too frightened to move. Then she pulled out the meat and threw some to the lion. He ate it and walked away among the trees.

The next day she fed the lion again in the same way. This went on for many days until the woman came out of hiding and began to go nearer, and still nearer, to the lion while he was eating. At last there came a day when he took the meat from her hand. Then, while the lion was at his meal, she was able to touch his body with the tips of her fingers—and pull out one single hair.

Then she ran quickly to the wise old man and begged him to make up the medicine at once.

He was amazed to see her with the hair of the lion. He questioned her carefully about what she had done until he was sure that her story was true. Then he said: "My child, I have no medicine for your husband. But I have advice for you.

"I see that you have pulled a hair from a living lion. It was a dangerous and fearful thing to do, needing patience and courage and care. Surely you who have done this thing can treat your husband reasonably and live with him happily.

"Just as you treated the lion with care and patience," said the old man, "now treat your husband in the same way. Do not be angry with him, for this will only make him worse. Instead, speak gently to him and give him advice. Tell him he has great responsibilities. Share his problems and make him feel he is wanted. Then see what happens."

The woman thanked him and went home. She did as he had told her, and slowly her husband's character was changed. He grew into a good man, who loved his wife and his home, and their life together was happy to the end of their days.

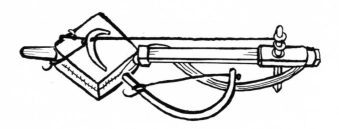

MESFIN HABTE-MARIAM was a student at Haile Selassie I University in Addis Ababa when he began to collect and translate the stories for this book. He has written both poetry and fiction in Amharic, and he remembered many Amharic folktales. Some of the stories had been told to him by his mother at home, and he had heard others from teachers and school friends. Later, while he was teaching at a school in Sidamo, he persuaded his own students to tell him stories from that part of the country. It was his hope that the collection of tales would reflect some of the beliefs and values of Ethiopians.

CHRISTINE PRICE has written and illustrated a number of children's books and is particularly interested in folklore. She has created picture books based on folktales and folk songs and also has made recordings of traditional stories from various countries, including two records of some of the tales from *The Rich Man and the Singer*. The idea for this book was born during a first visit to Ethiopia in 1968. She frequently travels abroad, usually with a book in mind. Between her journeys she lives among the Green Mountains of Vermont.